To my parents Rosamond and
Barton Myers Lloyd—S. W.

To my family, thank you for your support—A. R. D.

Published by Charlesbridge
85 Main Street
Watertown, MA 02472
(617) 926-0329
www.charlesbridge.com

Library of Congress Cataloging-in-Publication Data
Wolf, Sallie.
    Truck stuck / Sallie Wolf ; illustrated by Andy Robert Davies.
        p. cm.
    Summary: Illustrations and simple rhyming text tell the story
of a big truck that gets stuck under a bridge.
    ISBN 978-1-58089-119-6 (reinforced for library use)
    [1. Trucks—Fiction. 2. Vehicles—Fiction. 3. Stories in rhyme.]
I. Davies, Andy Robert, ill. II. Title.
PZ8.3.W82St 2008
[E]—dc22   2007002282

Illustrations done in pen and ink, then manipulated electronically.
Display type and text type set in Futura created by
Paul Renn of Bauhaus and Neue Grotesk
Color separations by Chroma Graphics, Singapore
Printed and bound by Regent Publishing Services
Production supervision by Brian G. Walker
Designed by Susan Mallory Sherman

Big truck.

Viaduct.
Uh-oh. Too low.
Stop, truck!

Truck stuck.

Let us through—we're stuck, too!
Jobs to do.

Recycling truck, excavator,

Street sweeper,   tree chipper,

delivery van, produce man.

Let us pass. Step on the gas!

Phones to fix.   Concrete to mix.

Lawns to mow.   Scouts on the go.

BIG tow truck,
yellow and green,
on the scene.
Let us through!

Back up, truck.
Unstuck.